W9-CAW-916

DON'T LOOK NOW

ED BRIANT

A NEAL PORTER BOOK . ROARING BROOK PRESS . NEW YORK

For Nat

"By this good light, this is a very shallow monster!"
William Shakespeare, *The Tempest*

Copyright © 2009 by Ed Briant
A Neal Porter Book
Published by Roaring Brook Press
Roaring Brook Press is a division of Holtzbrinck Publishing Holdings Limited Partnership
175 Fifth Avenue, New York, New York 10010
All rights reserved
www.roaringbrookpress.com

Distributed in Canada by H. B. Fenn and Company, Ltd.

Cataloging-in-Publication Data is on file at the Library of Congress.
ISBN-13: 978-1-59643-345-8
ISBN-10: 1-59643-345-0

Roaring Brook Press books are available for special promotions and premiums.
For details contact: Director of Special Markets, Holtzbrinck Publishers.

Printed in China
Book design by Barbara Grzeslo
First edition May 2009
2 4 6 8 10 9 7 5 3 1

DON'T LOOK NOW BUT THERE'S A...

DUH!

ICE CREAM!

DUH!

CLATTER

CRAA...

...ACK!

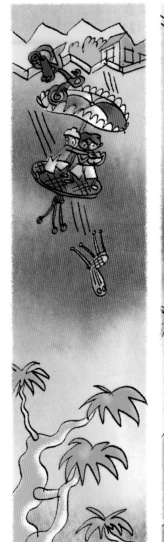

FLAP

FLIT

FLUP

RUMBLE

BWAAAAH...

POP

GASP

DON'T LOOK NOW BUT THERE'S A...